CALICO ILLUSTRATED CLASSICS
Charles Dickens's

Great Expectations

ADAPTED BY: Jan Fields
ILLUSTRATED BY: Patricia Castelao

magic
wagon

visit us at www.abdopublishing.com

Published by Magic Wagon, a division of the ABDO Group,
8000 West 78th Street, Edina, Minnesota 55439. Copyright
© 2010 by Abdo Consulting Group, Inc. International copyrights
reserved in all countries. All rights reserved. No part of this book
may be reproduced in any form without written permission from
the publisher.

Calico Chapter Books™ is a trademark and logo of Magic Wagon.

Printed in the United States of America, Melrose Park, Illinois.
102009
012010

 PRINTED ON RECYCLED PAPER

Original text by Charles Dickens
Adapted by Jan Fields
Illustrated by Patricia Castelao
Edited by Stephanie Hedlund and Rochelle Baltzer
Cover and interior design by Abbey Fitzgerald

Library of Congress Cataloging-in-Publication Data
Fields, Jan.
  Great expectations / adapted by Jan Fields ; illustrated by Patricia
Castelao ; based upon the works of Charles Dickens.
     p. cm. -- (Calico illustrated classics)
  ISBN 978-1-60270-706-1
  [1. Orphans--Fiction. 2. Coming of age--Fiction. 3. Great Britain--
History--19th century--Fiction.] I. Castelao, Patricia, ill. II. Dickens,
Charles, 1812-1870. Great expectations. III. Title.
  PZ7.F479177Gr 2010
  [Fic]--dc22
                                                    2009036520

Table of Contents

Pip

I never met my parents or my five brothers. I know only what little my sister told me. I have my father's name, Philip Pirrip, but have never worn it. When I was small, all I could say of the name was "Pip." Thus Pip I named myself, and Pip I am called.

One cold Christmas Eve, I visited the graveyard. I often came to read the tombstones of my family, looking for clues to who they were. My father's square stone made me certain he was a stout man. I looked down the row of neatly lined brothers that I would never meet. I began to cry.

"Keep still or I'll cut your throat!" A man rose from among the graves. He wore filthy, wet clothes and an iron cuff on one leg. He seized me by the chin and demanded, "What's your name?"

"Pip, sir," I whispered.

The man turned me upside down and emptied my pockets. A piece of bread fell out and he grabbed it before dumping me on a high tombstone.

He wolfed down the bread and stared at me again. "Where is your mother?"

I pointed. "There, sir!"

He jumped up and ran a few steps, then looked over his shoulder.

"There, sir!" I pointed at the tombstone. "*Also Georgiana*. That's my mother."

"Oh," he said, coming back. "And is that your father beside your mother?"

"Yes, sir."

He asked where I lived. I told him I lived with the village blacksmith.

"Blacksmith, eh?" He looked down at his leg, then he grabbed me by the arms and tilted me backward. "Bring me a file and some food in the morning."

He gave me a shake and I nodded.

"If you say a word about this," he growled, "I will cut out your heart and liver and roast them for dinner."

He gave me another shake. "There's a young man with me who is good at getting to a boy's heart and liver. A boy may be warm in his bed, tucked up and safe, but that young man will creep in. Don't fail to bring what I ask. Now get you home!"

He set me down and limped away through the gravestones, hugging his shivering body. Nettles and brambles caught at his clothes like the hands of dead people stretching up from the graves.

I looked around for the horrible young man. When I saw no sign of him, I ran home without stopping.

When I arrived home, the blacksmith forge was shut up and Joe was sitting alone in the

kitchen. I was pleased but nervous to see my sister absent.

Our neighbors frequently praised my sister for bringing me up "by hand." She had a hard and heavy hand. She was tall and bony and most always wore a coarse apron with the bib front stuck full of pins and needles like armor.

Joe was as different from his wife as storm is from sunshine. A strong man in body but sweet in nature, he paid hard for marrying my sister.

"Mrs. Joe is looking for you," Joe said. "She's due back. Best hide behind the door."

I took his advice but when my sister threw open the door, she knew what kept it from hitting the wall. She hauled me out and threw me at Joe. Joe slipped me behind him. I'm sure she would have snatched me again if he weren't such a stout wall.

"Where have you been while I've worried and fretted?" she demanded.

"The graveyard."

"Graveyard!" she grumbled. "The two of you

will drive me to the graveyard one day. What a pair you'd be without me!"

My sister then cut our nightly bread and butter. Though I was hungry, I knew I must hide my bread for the graveyard man and his terrifying partner.

Joe looked at me as I sat holding my untouched bread. Finally he turned his head and I slipped the bread down the leg of my pants. When Joe looked again, his eyes widened in alarm.

"Pip, you mustn't gobble your bread like that," he said, shaking his head. "It's a mercy you ain't gobbled yourself to death."

"Been gobbling his food has he?" cried my sister. She grabbed me by the hair and said the most awful of words, "You'll need a dose."

My sister was fond of a home remedy of tar and water that she believed cured anything. On this particular evening, my case demanded a pint of it poured down my throat. Joe got off with half of a pint.

I slipped away during his dosing and hid my guilty bread in my tiny bedroom. Then just before bed, I heard guns in the distance. "Another convict off," Joe said.

I was on fire with questions. What convicts did he mean? Where had they come from? Who was firing at them?

My sister glared at me. "From the prison ships in the river," she snapped.

I wondered aloud about who was put into prison ships and why they might be put there. My sister flew into a rant about how the murderers and robbers aboard the ship began their evil ways by asking too many questions. Then she sent me to bed.

I barely got any sleep, knowing I must rob the pantry at dawn. When the black of night turned to gray, I grabbed a load of food, nearly at random in my panic over being caught. Then I took a file from the forge and ran for the misty marshes.

CHAPTER 2

My Convict

I raced to meet the convict through the chilly fog. I jumped at every sound, certain my life as a thief would soon be found out. I spotted a man, folded upon himself with his back to me and head down as if asleep.

I touched him on the shoulder and he leaped to his feet and spun to face me. Though he wore the same gray clothes and the same thick leg iron, this was not my convict. I knew instantly it must be the young man who enjoyed cutting up boys.

I jumped back as the man took a weak swing at me. He stumbled as he missed. Then, he rushed past me into the mist.

Grateful to have my liver still inside me, I walked on. Soon I spotted the right man. He snatched my bundle and began cramming food into his mouth.

"You brought no one with you?" the man muttered around a mouthful of pork pie.

"No, sir!" The food disappeared at an amazing rate. "Will you not leave some for the young man?" I asked.

The man looked at me, puzzled, then laughed. "He only wants a boy's liver."

"He looked hungry," I said, shivering.

"When did you see him? Where did you see him? What did you see, boy?"

I pointed. "A man, dressed like you but with a hat. He had a badly bruised face and sat sleeping. I thought he was you."

"Bruised? Here?" The man struck his own cheek hard with the flat of his hand. I nodded.

The man dropped to the ground and stuffed the remaining bits of food into his shirt. He then filed at his leg iron like a madman. Since he took no more notice of me, I felt it best to go.

I half expected to be met at my sister's kitchen by a constable. Instead, I found Mrs. Joe preparing for her annual Christmas party.

"Where have you been?" she greeted me. "I'd like to be out and about. But I'm only a slave to you and that blacksmith and never get to take my apron off."

Mrs. Joe sent Joe and me to put on our best, most uncomfortable clothes. We finished that struggle just in time for the arrival of the guests. There were four: our church clerk, Mr. Wopsle, the wheel maker, Mr. Hubble, and his wife, and Joe's well-to-do uncle.

"The compliments of the season!" Uncle Pumblechook cried. Then we settled to a yearly tradition—criticizing my faults over dinner.

This was an activity taken up by everyone except Joe. Instead, he poured extra gravy on my dish at each remark to help me feel better. Soon I was judged ungrateful, vicious, and greedy, and my dish was a swamp of gravy.

Finally, my sister stood to announce that everyone must have some tasty pork pie. At this, I nearly yelped in terror as I remembered the face of the convict crammed with pork pie.

I fled the room but got no farther than the front door. When I opened it, I faced a party of soldiers. The moment of my arrest had surely come.

Our guests leaped to their feet at the sight of the soldiers. Just then my sister stormed into the kitchen calling, "My pie is gone!

Hunting

"Excuse me," called the sergeant, looking round at our stiffly dressed group. "We are on the king's business. Where is the blacksmith?"

My sister hated the idea of Joe being wanted for anything. She snapped, "What might you want with him?"

The sergeant bowed slightly and my sister warmed at his charming manner. "Speaking for the king." He held up the handcuffs. "The lock of one of these has gone wrong. Will you look at them?"

Joe looked. He said he would need to light his forge but could fix the cuffs in a couple of hours. While Joe set about the repair, the soldiers mingled with my sister's guests.

My sister became positively delighted and passed out refreshments. No more was said of the pie since the soldiers proved so much more interesting.

I heard Mr. Wopsle inquire about the soldiers' mission. The sergeant told him they were hunting two convicts hidden in the marsh.

When Joe finished the job, he asked if he and I might go with the soldiers to see the hunt. Mr. Wopsle added that he would like to join in also.

And so we were off into the bitter, sleety cold. The sergeant gave us sharp orders not to speak once we reached the marshes. Joe carried me on his back. I whispered to him that I hoped they'd not find the convicts. Joe agreed.

Suddenly I realized that the convicts would think I had led the soldiers to them. I felt much the worse for it. We trudged along for an endless while, when a shout in the distance set us to running that way.

As we drew close, we heard two voices along with the sounds of struggle. One shouted,

"Murder! Help!" While the other bellowed, "Convicts! The runaway convicts are here!"

Finally the soldiers scrambled into a ditch where two men fought—I recognized them both immediately. The sergeant shouted, "Surrender you two!"

"I caught him," my convict shouted. "I caught him for you!"

"Little good it will do you," the sergeant said. "Handcuff them."

My convict threw back his head and laughed. "It does me good enough. I know I took him. He knows it. That's enough." He pointed to his leg, bare of the iron. "I was free and could have fled, but I'd not let the likes of him escape."

The other convict leaned on the soldiers and panted, "Take notice, he tried to murder me."

"Liar," my convict spat.

"Enough chatter," the sergeant said. "You two are expected at the prison boat."

It was then that my convict spotted me. I tried to let him know that I was no rat. He gave me barely a glance. We marched for at least an hour and reached a rough wooden hut near the river where the soldiers handed over the prisoners.

My convict turned suddenly then to the sergeant and said, "I want to say something. I stole food from a house in the village yonder. At the home of the blacksmith. I took a pie— a whole pie."

The sergeant turned to Joe and asked, "Did you miss such things—food, a pie?"

Joe said that my sister had mentioned such a loss. The convict looked straight at him and apologized for eating our pie.

"You were welcome to it," Joe said. "We'd have no one starve to death, would we, Pip?"

The man turned away then without mention of my part in the loss of the pie. He was loaded into a small boat to be rowed out to the prison barge. And so he was gone and we were left to head for home, cold and tired.

Chapter 4

Miss Havisham

My conscience bothered me over my part in the Christmas adventure. Over the next year, I decided several times to confide in Joe, but I did not. I feared Joe would think poorly of me.

All my life, I knew I would be Joe's apprentice someday. In the meanwhile, I did any chores thrust at me. My sister felt hard work was proof against being pampered.

I was schooled by Mr. Wopsle's great aunt. There, I mainly learned that the great aunt could fall asleep in nearly any position. During her sudden naps, Biddy, the great aunt's granddaughter, taught me most of my letters and what little reading I could do. Biddy was an orphan too and brought up by hand.

And so my life was laid out. Until one day, an announcement from Uncle Pumblechook and my sister brought a startling change.

"Miss Havisham has asked for a boy to come and visit her," my sister announced gesturing at me. "This boy will do."

Everyone knew of Miss Havisham. She was old and grim and very rich. She never left her crumbling mansion known as Satis House.

We were informed that this great wonder had come about because Uncle Pumblechook was a tenant of Miss Havisham. The old woman had asked about a boy when Joe's uncle had come round the house to pay his rent.

It was decided—through no input from Joe or me—that I would go home with Uncle Pumblechook, spend the night, and be delivered to Miss Havisham in the morning.

"This boy's fortune may be made by this!" my sister insisted. Then she dragged me off to be scrubbed, soaked, and thumped. I was stuffed into my most uncomfortable clothes and delivered to Uncle Pumblechook. That night I slept in his attic space where the rafters nearly touched my nose.

The next morning, Uncle Pumblechook helped my schooling by making me do sums during breakfast. Too soon, we were off to Miss Havisham's huge brick house.

Several windows in the great house had been bricked over and the whole place had a great many iron bars to it. We rang the bell and waited.

A pretty young lady of about my age let me in. Then, she coldly dismissed Uncle Pumblechook and relocked the gate. We crossed the clean but cracked and weedy courtyard. I heard a great wind roaring through the long-neglected buildings.

I followed the girl into the house and through dark passages. Finally she stopped at a door and said, "Go in."

"After you, miss," I said.

"Foolish boy," she sniffed as she turned to walk away. "I am not going in."

Alone in the dark, I knocked and was told to come in. I entered a large room that was lit by candles. An old woman in a white dress and veil sat at a dressing table. She was surrounded by half-packed trunks with fine dresses draped over them. I noticed she wore only one white shoe, though the other lay nearby.

The woman was so old and thin that she looked like a skeleton dressed in fine clothes. She peered at me with dark eyes and said, "Who is it?"

"Pip, ma'am. Mr. Pumblechook's boy."

She waved me nearer and said, "I've not seen the sun since before you were born." She reached her bony hands to the bodice of her dress. "What do I touch here?"

"Your heart," I said.

"Broken," she crowed, then she dropped her hands. "I want entertainment—play!"

I stood staring and confused until the old woman grew annoyed. "Call Estella!"

The beautiful girl swept back into the room with her candle. Miss Havisham called her over and held jewels up to her pretty brown hair and fair skin.

"Your own—someday—to use well," the old woman said. "Play cards with the boy."

"He's a common laboring boy!" Estella cried.

"Well?" asked the old woman. "You can break his heart."

And so we played while the old woman watched us like a propped corpse. Estella criticized everything about me over the game. "He calls the knaves *Jacks*. He has coarse hands. Look how thick his boots are!"

Her disgust with me was so clear in the air that I caught it like a cold. I hated my hands, my boots, my way of speaking.

"She says much of you," Miss Havisham observed. "What do you say of her? Tell me in my ear."

I told Miss Havisham that I found Estella very proud, very pretty, and very insulting. I added that I had no interest in seeing her again and would like to go home.

"Play the game out," Miss Havisham said. "You will go soon."

I finished the game and Estella won. She

threw the cards down as if even winning was too common for her.

"Come again in six days," Miss Havisham instructed, then she turned to Estella. "Take him down and feed him."

Estella led me downstairs and gave me bread and meat with as little interest as she might feed a stray dog. I blinked shamed tears until the girl was gone, then I gave full voice to my pain, kicking the wall as I cried.

Finally, Estella came back. She saw I'd been crying. She laughed at me and pushed me out through the gate, leaving me to a four-mile walk back to the forge.

My Work Began

My sister and Uncle Pumblechook pelted me with questions when I reached home. I made up wild stories until they turned their attention to dreaming of what Miss Havisham might do for my fortunes.

It was only to Joe that I told the real truth and my shame at being common. Joe was shocked to hear I'd lied and said, "Lies ain't no way out of being common. I figure uncommon has to start with being common and working your way out, just the way the alphabet starts at *A* and works its way to *Z*."

Joe's view on the alphabet set me to thinking that Biddy could help in my journey out of being common. So I sought all the learning I could from her, and she did as best she could.

After one such lesson, I trotted over to the public house where Joe often spent evenings. I spotted Joe speaking with a stranger. The stranger asked questions about our names and things one might find in the marshes. Then the stranger pulled a file out of his inner pocket and used it to stir his drink.

When we rose to go home, the man said he had a shilling for me and handed me a coin and some crumpled paper. The paper turned out to be two one pound notes!

With these adventures behind me, I returned to Satis House at the appointed time. Estella let me in. She led me through the house and up the stairs, where we met a large man coming down.

He stopped and stared at me darkly. "What do we have here?"

"A boy," Estella snapped.

"I know about boys," he said. "Behave yourself!"

I followed Estella the rest of the way and entered Miss Havisham's room as before. I stood still and waited until she looked at me. "Are you ready to play?"

"I don't think I am, ma'am."

"Then are you willing to work?"

This I agreed to quickly and Miss Havisham commanded that I wait for her in the room across the hall. I went to the room and found it quite as dark as the rest of the house. The wintery candles on the mantle lit the darkness only slightly.

The room was covered with dust and mold. A long table took up the center of the room, as if for a feast. Some hulking thing sat in the middle of the table. Spiders scuttled to and from the hulk as if it were the central meeting place of the spider community.

I jumped as a hand rested on my shoulder. Miss Havisham pointed toward the table with

the tip of her cane. "My wedding cake," she said.

I had no answer to that. Miss Havisham looked around the room and demanded, "Walk me, walk me!"

And so my work began. On every visit after that, I would walk Miss Havisham around the room. During these walks, she would ask me questions about my life and situation. I answered as best I could.

Afterward, I would play cards with Estella. I grew better at cards but not at understanding the proud and beautiful girl. Some days she treated me with the deepest scorn. On some visits she acted almost as if she were fond of me, as if I were a pet. As each visit piled one on another, I grew more unhappy with who I was.

During one walk around the room, Miss Havisham noted several times that I had grown. She announced, "You had better be apprenticed at once. Have Gargery bring you here and bring the papers for your apprenticeship."

And so he did and me with him. Joe was in a state of wretched nerves. He seemed even more common and foolish and my shame grew greater than ever before. Estella laughed at him, but Miss Havisham was not unkind.

"Pip has been a good boy," Miss Havisham said. "He has earned the right to pay for his apprenticeship and so here is the pay." She handed Joe twenty-five guineas. "As an honest man you'll expect no less and no more."

And with that she dismissed us, telling me that I was done at her house. "Gargery is your master now," she said.

We returned to my sister and Uncle Pumblechook, who waited always for news of Miss Havisham. My sister was delighted with the money. Uncle Pumblechook, however, insisted on a more formal arrangement for my apprenticeship. He dragged me like a captured criminal to the town hall for my papers to be signed. And thus I began as Joe's apprentice.

Changes

Until meeting Miss Havisham and Estella, I had thought our tiny parlor elegant. I had looked at Joe's forge as the perfect proof of adulthood. But now I despised it all and lived in terror of Estella seeing my home and my work.

I thought often of Estella. My need to see her grew almost painfully strong. One day I asked Joe's leave so that I might take a half day to visit.

"Miss Havisham might be thinking you want something," Joe warned. "If you remember, she said that was all."

"I won't ask for anything," I said. "She'll see."

"Maybe," Joe said, "and maybe not." But he agreed to my time off and so the day was set for my visit.

Joe had employed a journeyman to help at the forge for as long as I could remember. Dolge Orlick became openly jealous once I was formally apprenticed to Joe.

When Orlick heard of my half-day vacation, he demanded his own and Joe agreed. My sister burst in then, ranting about the foolishness of paying wages to lazy workers.

My sister and Orlick bellowed at one another until Joe stepped in. All seemed quiet by the time I left. I hurried the four miles to Miss Havisham's mansion. There I found a new gatekeeper, Miss Havisham's cousin, Miss Pocket.

Miss Pocket lacked no skill in making me feel unwanted. It was clear she would have turned me away if she dared. Instead, I found myself in the old woman's unchanging room.

"What do you want?" Miss Havisham demanded.

"Only to tell you that I am doing well," I said. "And to thank you."

Seeing that I truly wasn't there to ask for anything, Miss Havisham softened. She said I should visit again on my birthday.

She caught me looking around and said, "Estella is abroad. I sent her to be educated as a lady. She is much admired for her beauty." Seeing my disappointment, she laughed and sent me away.

On my walk home, I ran into Mr. Wopsle. Then we came upon Orlick, who joined us in our walk. When we reached the public house, Mr. Wopsle popped in. He rushed out again and yelled, "There's something wrong at your house, Pip. Run home now!"

I ran. At the house I found my sister lying on the bare boards. Someone had knocked her hard on the head. No one saw the attack.

I knew the authorities suspected Joe for a long time. But my own suspicions turned toward Orlick.

My sister was ill for many days and though she grew stronger, she was changed. She could not speak clearly. She communicated a bit with chalk marks on a slate. She became quiet and patient, with particular interest in Orlick's good opinion. She often called for him through her marks.

We had a rough time until dear Biddy came to take care of us. Biddy was especially good at understanding my sister's slate marks. Under Biddy's care, we grew as cheerful and content as possible.

As good as Biddy was at housekeeping and teaching, she was even better at listening. I took to taking long walks with her, talking about my dreams.

"Biddy," I said, "I want to be a gentleman."

"Don't you think you're happier as you are?" she asked.

I huffed. "I am disgusted with my calling and with my life."

I told her about Estella and how I longed to be a gentleman and win her over. Biddy was kind but clearly thought my longings foolish.

After our talk, I found myself more confused than ever. Some days I was happy at the forge and admiring of Biddy's quick mind and kind heart. Other days, I could think of nothing but Estella and I was miserable again.

Pip, a Gentleman

One night, Joe and I were at the public house listening to Mr. Wopsle rant about a murder case in the newspaper. A stranger came up and scolded Mr. Wopsle for making unfair assumptions.

The man soon had Wopsle totally speechless, something we'd not often seen. Then the stranger turned to the rest of us and asked for Joseph Gargery.

"Here," Joe said.

"And you have an apprentice known as Pip," the man said. "Is he here?"

"I am," I cried. And it was then that I recognized the man as the stranger on the stairs at Miss Havisham's house those years before.

The man said he would like to speak to us privately. So we walked home, no one speaking until we were settled in the parlor.

"My name is Jaggers," the man announced. "I have come to make an offer that I would not make were it up to me—it is not. I am here on behalf of another whose name will not be mentioned."

Jaggers then asked Joe if he would release me from my bond as an apprentice if something more for my good came along. Joe agreed immediately.

Mr. Jaggers then turned to me. "It is the desire of your anonymous benefactor that you be brought up as a gentleman. You are a man of great expectations."

I stared in stunned silence as Jaggers outlined the conditions. I must never ask the name of my benefactor or make public any guesses about the person's identity. I was to keep the name "Pip." And I was to go to London, where Mr. Matthew Pocket would be my tutor.

Mr. Pocket was another relative of Miss Havisham, so I felt that was proof. Miss Havisham must intend to make me a gentleman fit for Estella.

"You will need clothes," Jaggers said. "Not working clothes, but clothes fitting a young man of great expectations." He opened a purse and counted out twenty guineas for their purchase. Soon after, he left.

Both Joe and Biddy congratulated me heartily but with sadness. They kept saying, "Pip, a gentleman . . ." with such wonder and disbelief that I became quite annoyed.

Preparations for leaving kept me busy. First I had to order clothes, so I went to the village tailor. Mr. Trabb seemed content to chat with me over his breakfast as if my needs were less than his need for toast and butter. Then I mentioned my good fortune.

Mr. Trabb hopped up and quickly led me into the shop proper. He had his assistant bring out fine cloth, which he recommended for different situations. After I chose, he promised to have my new things finished quickly.

When my new clothes were finally done, I slipped into them and went straightaway to visit Miss Havisham. Miss Pocket was clearly shocked to see me in my new suit, but it did not improve her manners.

"Good gracious!" she cried. "What do you want?"

I told her I wanted to see Miss Havisham. She left me waiting at the gate while she learned whether Miss Havisham wanted to see me. She did.

I found Miss Havisham pacing around the great room that held her wedding cake. "I leave for London tomorrow," I said. "I wanted to say good-bye."

"Yes, I have seen Mr. Jaggers," the old woman said. Then she encouraged me to repeat each detail of my good fortune, while Miss Pocket grew paler and more visibly jealous.

Finally Miss Havisham bid me good-bye. And so I left my fairy godmother, with both hands on her cane and the crumbling cake beside her.

When the day came for my leaving, I kissed Biddy and my sister, who laughed. I threw my arms around Joe. Then I left.

The journey to London took about five hours. Had I not been convinced that London held the very best of everything, I might have found it dirty, ugly, and narrow.

I went at once to Mr. Jaggers's rooms. As the lawyer was not yet back from court, I passed the time with a little walk. In the streets near his office, I heard Mr. Jaggers's name on many lips. Clearly, he was a man of fierce reputation.

When he finally arrived, he told me I would receive an allowance. "You are not limited to that," he said. "You'll find your credit good, and I'll keep my eye out that you don't let your debt run away from you."

He explained that my bills would be sent to his office and paid by his clerk, Wemmick.

After that, Mr. Wemmick walked me to the rooms belonging to my tutor's son. I would be staying with him until I met his father on Monday.

London

Mr. Wemmick had a face made of sharp angles with a thin, wide slit for a mouth. His small, black eyes glittered as he spoke. "Have you ever been to London before?"

"No," I said. "Is it a very wicked place?"

"Like many others full of people," he said. "People who will kill you if there is profit in it."

I then asked him several questions about my tutor.

"Why, you're a regular cross-examiner!" he said in clear approval, though I noticed he did little to answer my questions.

When we reached Barnard's Inn, I offered him my hand, which clearly startled him. He said that he'd quite gotten out of the habit, except with clients on their way to execution.

"As I keep the cash for Mr. Jaggers," Wemmick said, shaking my hand, "we shall most likely meet pretty often. Good day."

I found myself alone outside the rooms of Herbert Pocket. A sign on the door to the rooms said, "Back soon." After standing awhile, I decided Mr. Pocket's idea of soon and mine were far different.

I occupied myself with writing on a filthy window with my finger. I had just finished filling every pane with my name when I heard footsteps on the stairs.

Mr. Pocket gushed with apology. He handed me parcels of food he had bought for my arrival so he could wrestle open the door. I stared at him without speaking. I had met him before.

I had run across him in the overgrown garden of Miss Havisham's house during one of my visits. He had appeared like a ghost and demanded that we fight. He'd stripped to the waist, and we'd boxed a bit. He was a dreadful fighter and I'd knocked him around. Now he was to be my roommate!

Finally the door gave and Mr. Pocket tumbled into the room. He turned back to me to collect the packages. In that moment I saw him make the same connection I had made.

"You're the prowling boy!" he cried.

"And you," I said, "are the pale young gentleman." We stared at one another for a moment, then burst out laughing.

"I never saw you there again," I mentioned.

"Oh, I was only there on a trial visit," Mr. Pocket said cheerfully. "Miss Havisham didn't take to me. I suspect I was being considered as a match for Estella. She was quite a witch."

"Miss Havisham?" I asked.

"Well, yes, but that's not who I meant," he said. "Estella was most unpleasant. But then Miss Havisham raised her to wreak havoc on the male sex."

"Why?" I asked, totally confused.

"Ah, now there's a story," he said. "Let's have it over dinner."

I liked Herbert Pocket straightaway. I could tell he would never do anything mean or sneaky. Since he was so open and kind, I found myself filling the time before dinner with my own life story.

At the completion of my story, he asked me to call him Herbert. Then he announced that he would call me Handel. This nickname came from a composer who wrote a piece of music about a blacksmith. I agreed since it seemed to make him happy.

Dinner arrived then and we ate with enthusiasm. I think it had extra flavor by being my first meal in London. As we ate, I asked him to tell me immediately if he saw me do anything common.

"At once," Herbert said, adding that one did not usually put a knife in one's mouth—for fear of accidents.

"And many people here hold their spoon underhand instead of overhand, which surprisingly makes it much easier to reach your mouth. And that is the goal."

His suggestions were so lively and friendly that we both laughed and I hardly minded at all. Soon the topic changed to Miss Havisham and Estella.

"Now," he said, "Miss Havisham was a spoiled child. Her mother died when she was an infant, and her father never told her *no*. He was very rich and very proud and his daughter was as well. Oh, and your dinner napkin ought not to go in your glass."

I pulled out the napkin at once and thanked Herbert again.

"According to my father, a showy man appeared soon after her father died and began to court Miss Havisham. My father said the man managed to charm her completely. She gave him great sums of money.

"A wedding day was set. The day came, but not the man. He sent a note instead."

"Which she read while she was dressing for the wedding?" I asked.

"Yes," Herbert said, "and at that hour she stopped all the clocks, froze time in her house completely. And she has never since looked upon the light of day."

"I wonder why the man didn't marry her and get all her money," I pondered.

"Some say he may have been married already."

"And whose child is Estella?" I asked.

"I don't know. She's adopted," Herbert said. "She's been raised to take Miss Havisham's revenge upon men."

At that point, the conversation strayed to Herbert. He said he would truly love to be in shipping, trading all over the world. And I hoped great success for him, no matter how unlikely it seemed.

CHAPTER 9

Visiting

Herbert showed me a bit more of London in the days ahead. Then he took me to meet his father. I found the Pocket house bustling with children. They were always tumbling over one another.

Mrs. Pocket seemed to mother best by avoiding the children entirely. She appeared startled whenever one thrust itself upon her.

Mr. Pocket was a gray-haired gentleman in a state of constant bewilderment. He reminded me of Herbert. I liked him at once.

I learned I was to join two other young men under Mr. Pocket's tutoring: Drummle and Startop. Drummle had some link with royalty and considered himself better than the rest of us. But Startop was a cheerful young man with a great devotion to his mother.

My tutoring would not include useful training to prepare for an occupation. Instead, I was merely to learn to be a gentleman.

After a few weeks, I received two unusual dinner invitations. The first was from Mr. Jaggers's clerk, Wemmick, and the second from Mr. Jaggers himself.

I met Mr. Wemmick at the office and walked home with him. With each block we walked, Mr. Wemmick seemed to shed some of the stiffness of the office. When we finally reached his small house, he glowed with good cheer.

Mr. Wemmick's aged father lived with him. The old man was deaf as a stone but greeted me cheerfully. Wemmick showed me around, explaining that he had done all his own engineering, plumbing, gardening, and carpentry. The result was an odd little house with a drawbridge, a peculiar fountain, and a great coziness.

From this unusual visit, I came to understand that people are often not just one thing—they can change. The serious Mr. Wemmick of the lawyer's office became the cheerful Mr. Wemmick at home.

The dinner with Mr. Jaggers showed me just the opposite. He was the same at home as in the office. His rooms were gloomy and ill-kept, but the food was good.

Jaggers had asked that I bring Drummle and Startop with me. He seemed to prefer Drummle over the rest of us and encouraged his surly behavior throughout the dinner.

Still, the most unusual thing about the dinner was Mr. Jaggers's housekeeper. Her behavior toward Mr. Jaggers seemed overly attentive, almost fearful.

At one point, Drummle, Startop, and I were engaged in a silly display of showing off our muscles. None of us could compete with Drummle, who was a tall, stout fellow. Mr. Jaggers suddenly reached out and snatched his

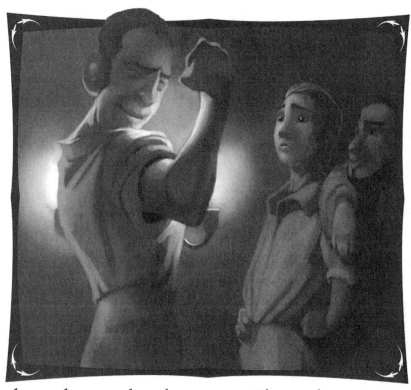

housekeeper by the arm. "Show them your wrists, Molly," he said.

"Master," she murmered. "Please."

"Show them," he demanded.

She showed her hands and wrists, one deeply scarred. "There's power here," Jaggers said. "Few men have the power this woman has." With that, he let her go and us as well, sending us home for the night.

Before I left, I mentioned his fascination with Drummle. "I'm glad you like him, sir," I said. "But I don't."

"No," Mr. Jaggers said. "Stay clear of him if you can. Good night, Pip."

A month later, Drummle's time with us was up and he went home. I missed him not a bit.

⚜

As odd things come in threes, it was not long after these two dinner experiences that I had a third surprise, a visit from Joe Gargery.

I wish I could say I was pleased by it. I should have been, but I would have paid Joe to stay away if I dared. I didn't want him in my new place and my new life.

I was in a state of great nerves when he arrived. I knew it was him by his heavy tread upon the stairs. I thought he would never finish wiping his feet on the mat. But eventually he did come in and shook my hand as if it were the handle of a well pump.

I offered to take his hat, but he would not give it up. Instead he held it between us like a shield until the time came to sit and eat. Then he balanced the hat on the end of the fireplace mantle, where it fell on the floor several times.

At the table, Herbert asked, "Coffee or tea, Mr. Gargery?"

Joe sat as stiff as if he were cast in bronze. "Whichever is most agreeable to you, sir."

"Coffee then?" Herbert suggested.

"Thank you, sir," Joe said sadly. "Though don't you find it heats you up?"

"Say tea then," Herbert said and poured for us. Herbert put forth his best to make conversation with Joe, but my poor old friend twisted himself into spasms of words and sirs. He dropped more food than he ate. We were all grateful when the meal was over.

I thought I hid my feelings from Joe, but when finally it was just Joe and I alone, he said to me, "I'll not come again, sir."

"But of course you should," I said.

Joe just shook his great head. "I don't belong here, Pip. Not in these clothes or this place. If you want to see your old friend Joe again, come stick your head in at the forge. I'll be there."

He shuffled a bit then and added. "I have a message for you, Pip. Miss Havisham asked me to come see her. When I did, she told me Estella was coming home. She said to tell you that Estella would be glad to see you. And so I've told you."

He touched me then, gently on the forehead. "God bless you, dear old Pip," he said, then he went out.

I was quite overcome with everything he'd said. I stood staring for a long moment after him. When I finally came to myself and ran out, he was gone.

Love

Of course, I prepared to visit Estella immediately. I knew I should stay with Joe. I could mend some of the harm I had done. But I quickly talked myself out of that. Joe's forge was too far from Miss Havisham's house.

On the journey, two convicts and their guard rode atop our carriage for a while. It was not uncommon for prisoners to be carried from London this way. I recognized one of them instantly. It was the man who had stirred his tea with Joe's file and given me two pounds all those years ago. I hid my head, terrified he might recognize me, but he did not.

As the convicts rode, they talked about their destination. "I've been there just once," said the convict I recognized. "I was on an odd errand for a man I'd met on the prison barge. He pressed some notes upon me and told me to give them to a boy who had cared for him kindly."

The other convict laughed. "Don't tell me you did it?"

"I did."

"I wouldn't have," the laughing man said. "I would have kept them."

Discovering the answer to the mystery of the one pound notes did nothing to calm my nerves. I wanted no reminders of my past. I was a man of means now, not a boy frightened of shadows in a graveyard.

Though I kept to my decision not to visit Joe, I met with still more of the past on my visit home. As I hurried down the street away from the coach, the tailor's boy caught sight of me. He set to shadowing me with a group of friends. The boy strutted along behind me, crowing, "Don't know yah, don't know yah, 'pon my soul, don't know yah."

The boys' mocking laughter followed me for some blocks. I decided to post a note to the tailor immediately telling him I would not buy again from a man who would employ such a poorly behaved boy. And with that, I swept the boy from my mind and pressed on.

The third unpleasant shock of the day came when I arrived at Miss Havisham's and discovered she had a new gateman—Orlick!

"Have you left the forge?" I asked, too stunned for sensible speech.

"Do you see a forge?" Orlick asked. He showed me the little house in which he now lived as gateman. I spotted a thick club.

"Hereabouts can be dangerous with convicts and all going up and down the street," he said.

Setting Orlick to protect Estella made me feel cold. I decided that I would contact Mr. Jaggers right away and let him know Orlick was not a man to guard innocent women. And in that worried frame of mind, I hurried up to Miss Havisham's rooms.

I found the old lady much as I left her, at her dressing table with her spare shoe in her hand. A stranger attended her—an elegant woman.

"Well, Pip?" Miss Havisham said.

I looked closely at the other woman and saw it was my dear Estella—grown, elegant, and more beautiful.

"Do you find her much changed?" Miss Havisham asked.

I stammered and mumbled something vague. Miss Havisham asked Estella if she found me much changed.

"Very much," Estella said.

Estella and I soon slipped away to walk and talk. I found her less insulting but just as cold as in the past. I declared my love for her.

"I cannot love you, Pip," she said. "I have no heart, no kindness, no sentiment. I am what I was raised to be."

And with this, we rejoined Miss Havisham, who pulled me aside to command me in mad tones, "Love her, Pip. Love her though she'll pull your heart to bits."

I deeply feared I had no choice. Upon my return to London, I decided to talk with Herbert about my feelings.

"Herbert," I said one evening, "I love Estella."

"Yes," he said, leaning forward as if awaiting more.

"You act as though you knew that already," I said, surprised.

"My dear Handel," he said, "everyone who has ever heard the word *Estella* on your lips knows."

This stunned me and it took some moments to recover. "I believe Miss Havisham intends that I marry Estella."

"Is it a requirement of your inheritance?" he asked.

"Of course not."

"Then resist. Stay far away from her. Turn your feelings elsewhere," Herbert urged. "She'll break your heart over and over. It's her nature and her design."

I was shocked by Herbert's urgings, and we soon turned the conversation to other things. Herbert confided his great love for a girl named Clara.

"We are engaged," Herbert said. "But it's a secret."

Herbert's marriage was dependent upon a change in Herbert's own circumstances. Though a gentleman, Herbert had always been poor. Since living with me, I had led us both into unwise spending.

I had made hints that perhaps I could share some of my means with him, but Herbert would hear none of it. He was endlessly hopeful that he would find his place and position soon. Clearly it would need to be very soon, for the sum of our debt was great and growing.

I determined to keep my eye open for an opportunity for Herbert. He seemed to be advancing little from his own searches.

Soon, I received a note from Estella to meet her when she arrived in London. She wished me to help her to her destination just outside the city. Naturally I met her and made certain to provide every luxury available on such short notice.

"What is the purpose of this trip?" I asked.

"I am going to live with a lady who will introduce me around," Estella said. I knew she meant introductions to potential suitors.

"I suppose you will be glad of the admiration," I said, barely keeping the sulk out of my voice.

"I suppose," she said carelessly. I did notice that she was being unusually friendly. I hoped her feelings toward me were warming.

Estella

One evening, after a particularly depressing session of counting our bills, a note dropped through the letter slit. The note said my sister had died. My presence was expected at her funeral.

I had thought little of my sister since my move to London, but I found that I missed her. I sent a note to Joe, saying I would soon be there.

Joe greeted me warmly. Together we faced the funeral, where we were draped in yards of black fabric. Joe was forced to wear a black cape with a huge bow under his chin. The neighbors clearly thought well of the funeral procession, as they all stood in the street to watch us pass. I felt great relief when it was over.

Later, I mentioned to Biddy that I intended to come home more often now. Biddy could not stay with Joe and he would need my visits.

"Are you quite sure that you will come see him?" Biddy asked, disbelief plain on her face.

"Biddy, you shock me," I said, forgetting I had given Biddy good reason to doubt me.

I kept some distance from Biddy for the rest of my visit. When time came for me to leave, I shook Joe's hand warmly and nodded fondly at Biddy. Then I walked into the mist that lay on the early morning streets. I expect it looked a bit like I was disappearing from their lives. I hoped I was not.

I returned to London for my birthday. I had come of age. I met with Jaggers to learn of changes in my situation. I would receive more money now that I was old enough to look after it. Jaggers still would not share my benefactor's name.

Jaggers chided me on my mounting debt, then gave me a check for 500 pounds, telling me that I would receive such a check monthly. This was a great relief to me. With careful living, I could soon be out of debt.

I decided then that part of my money must go to helping Herbert. I had been a poor friend to enough people. It was time to show myself worthy of one. So I brought the subject up with Jaggers's clerk Wemmick. I visited him at home, for the work Wemmick thought poorly of charitable acts. I suspected the home Wemmick would approve of them. He did.

He agreed to put some thought and research into how I might help Herbert. Wemmick found a merchant in search of both capital and an eventual partner. It seemed the perfect situation for Herbert. We set about making it happen as secretly as possible.

I will never forget the joy on Herbert's face when he announced his new position. It was a joy that made me suspect that this was the reason fate had given me such great expectations.

I also spent time with Estella after my return to London. She had a great many admirers, including Bentley Drummle. I found this distasteful. Estella clearly cared no more for him than any of her other admirers, which gave me some comfort.

By-and-by, Estella asked me to accompany her on a visit to Miss Havisham. When we reached the house, Miss Havisham clung to Estella. She demanded details of Estella's admirers.

I realized then that this time in London was part of Miss Havisham's plan for Estella's life. She would break the hearts of young men until Miss Havisham's greed for revenge was fulfilled. Then Estella would be handed to me as wife, or so I hoped.

Throughout the visit, Miss Havisham clutched at Estella's arm and hair until Estella grew annoyed.

"What?" Miss Havisham demanded. "Are you tired of me?"

Estella looked coldly at her and then at the fire.

"You cold heart!" the old woman shouted.

"You scold me for being cold? I am what you have made me. What you wanted me to be. I cannot love anyone," Estella said. "You taught me too well."

At that, Miss Havisham waved me out of the room. I fretted as I walked the empty halls. If Estella truly could love no one, where did that leave me? When I finally returned to Miss Havisham's room, I found the crisis over.

When Estella returned again to London, I continued to see her and to suffer as she basked in her admirers.

At least Herbert thrived, growing more joyful with each passing day. Soon enough I found myself at twenty-three with the feeling I was on the edge of some great change, but I did not know when it would arrive or how.

A Stranger Arrives

One stormy night I was home alone. Business had called Herbert away for several days. Wind rushed up the river and shook the house as rain threw itself against the windows. The force of wind and rain blew out the lamps outside, making the darkness complete.

I was reading when I heard footsteps on the stairs. I was not expecting company in this weather and it was far too soon for Herbert's return.

I carried a lamp out the door of our rooms and lit the stairwell, where a stranger stood. His face lit up upon seeing mine. "Mr. Pip!"

"That is my name," I said, and I asked him his business. He said he would tell me but would

like to come in first. I stepped back into my rooms and the man followed. He was dressed coarsely in sailor's clothes. I knew of no one like him who should act so delighted at the sight of me. The mystery of it made me nervous, which the man must have seen.

"Of course, there's no reason for a better greeting," the man muttered. "You're not to blame for that. Neither of us is to blame for that."

Finally my worry boiled up. "Why do you, a stranger, come into my rooms at this time of night?" I demanded, taking a step toward him.

He grinned then, shaking his head with clear affection at my tone. "You're a game one. I'm glad you've grown up a game one. But I'd not take on the likes of me if I were you. You'd not like the result."

And it was with those words that time moved under me. I was in a graveyard in the bitter cold face-to-face with a desperate man. I knew who I faced—my convict.

With that realization, I reluctantly offered my hand. He grasped it and kissed it, shocking me deeply.

"You acted noble, my boy," the man said. "And I have never forgot it."

I thought he was only there to thank me and I calmed down a bit. I offered him a place by the fire to dry his clothes from the storm.

"You should drink something before you go," I said, not wanting him to think I wished him to stay. The man looked around him nodding and smiling, though dabbing at his eyes now and then.

"I received the money you sent long ago," I said. "The one pound notes. They were a fortune to me then."

"Good, good," he said. "And I see you have done well. May I ask how you have come to be a gentleman?"

"I was chosen," I said, "to receive an education and funds."

"Ah," he said, smiling again and nodding. "And might I guess the monthly amount of those funds? Shall I guess 500 pounds?"

My heart pounded in my chest with the realization that this man had come for more than to thank me. I wanted to make him stop speaking. I did not want to follow this conversation where it must go.

"And the guardian who has taken care of this," the man said. "Is his name Jaggers?"

With that, the room began to spin and I

could not catch my breath. The man leaped from his chair and helped me to the sofa, apologizing for the shock he had given me.

"Yes, Pip, dear boy," he said. "I have made a gentleman of you."

The man told me his name, Abel Magwitch. He said he had been exiled to Australia following the incident from my childhood. In Australia, he had worked tirelessly to make his fortune so he could invest it in making mine.

He praised my rooms, my clothes, and the jewelry and watch I wore. It was proof that all he had worked for had met success. He had made a gentleman.

"They mocked me," he said. "Those that thought they were better. They called me convict. And all the while I knew. I knew that you were becoming a gentleman. And now I've come to see it and to enjoy the sight."

It seemed more than I could take in. I asked him how long he meant to stay.

"I do not mean to leave," he said, then he

dropped his voice. "But we must be cautious, Pip. I was sent away for life and if I'm caught in London, they'll hang me."

At that, I rushed to close the shutters. I planned to hide his identity from the women who kept the rooms. We would say he was my uncle Provis.

Finally, he went to bed in Herbert's room and I was left to think about my life. I was not a gentleman raised as a match for Estella. Miss Havisham saw me only as practice for Estella's cold displays.

All that I was came from a convict. I had turned my back on Joe and Biddy at the whim of a convict. I looked at the things around me as if they dripped blood.

What crimes had driven the convict to Australia? What crimes might he yet commit? Whatever happened to him, I knew would happen to me as surely as if I were bound to his ankle with a shackle. This time, there would be no file to set us free.

Knowledge

The next day, I asked around to see who might have seen the arrival of my new uncle. The watchman said he had given my uncle and the man with him directions.

"A man was with him?" I asked.

"He seemed to be," the watchman said. "He came so soon after."

When asked, Provis had no explanation for a second man. "I came alone and there's no reason for any to look for me here," he said.

Since Herbert would soon be returning, I sought better clothes and lodging for my new uncle. I managed to get him the clothes of a gentleman farmer. But even in new clothing, he looked every inch a convict to me.

As quickly as I could, I visited Mr. Jaggers, to be certain of my convict's story. Nearly as soon as I began speaking, Mr. Jaggers put up a hand to stop me.

"I merely want to know," I said, "if information I have received is correct. Is my benefactor Abel Magwitch?"

"That is the man," Jaggers said. "Keep in mind that to my knowledge he is in Australia. I need only that knowledge."

I sank heavily into a chair. "I had always supposed it was Miss Havisham."

"It amused her for you to suppose it," Jaggers agreed. "I said nothing to lead you to that idea."

"No," I said, "I came there all on my own."

"Since Mr. Magwitch has informed you of his patronage," Jaggers said, "our business together is done. I have some monies left that will be handed over to you entirely. And we will see no more of each other. Good day, Pip." We shook hands and he looked hard at me until I left.

I barely slept or ate for the next five days as I awaited the return of Herbert. I needed someone to confide in, someone to help me make sense of what my life had become. Finally after dinner one evening, I heard the familiar footsteps on the stairs and Herbert burst into our rooms.

"Handel, I feel I have been gone a year," he declared, grabbing my hand and shaking it. Then he spotted Provis.

Provis rushed at him, pulling a small book from his pocket and thrusting it forward. "Take this in your right hand and swear."

Totally bewildered, Herbert did as asked. Provis shook his hand enthusiastically. I led Herbert closer to the fire, and we told him the whole of the secret of Abel Magwitch.

I kept my misgivings to myself until I had walked Provis to his own rooms, then I poured out my heart to Herbert. I couldn't possibly accept another cent of the man's money. I had no idea of the depth of evilness in his past.

"But what am I to do?" I cried. "I'm fit for nothing."

"I doubt that," Herbert said. "You might find yourself in a fine position. Look at me. Things didn't look good at all, and now I am working to become a partner at Clarriker's house!"

I would never tell Herbert the source of that good fortune was the same as the source of my present misery.

"You have a greater problem," Herbert said.

"What?"

"Clearly, you are what this man has lived for," Herbert said. "Seeing you succeed has been everything to him. Take that away, and I don't know what would happen."

Seeing my horror, Herbert added, "He might do himself harm or even turn himself in to be hanged. I think you'd not wish his death on your mind."

"No indeed," I said. "But what can I do?"

"You must get him out of England," Herbert said. "Go with him. Once he is safe, then you could tell him or leave him a note and come back."

"A good plan," I agreed. "But before I go abroad, I must see Estella and Miss Havisham. And I wish I knew exactly what Provis had done to receive a death sentence. I would rest easier on the trip if I knew he wouldn't cut out my liver in the night." I paused, working up my courage. "I must ask him point-blank."

"Then do," Herbert urged. "Ask him at breakfast tomorrow."

I worried all night about the horrors that awaited in my convict's story, but I was determined.

"Tell me, please," I said at the end of breakfast. "What brought about your imprisonment?" Provis reminded us of our sworn promise, then took out his pipe and began his tale.

Provis's Story

"I can tell you the bulk of my life quickly," Provis said. "In jail, out of jail, in jail, out of jail. I begged, I stole, and I worked when I could. Then I grew to be a man. I worked a bit more often and saw less time in jail."

Provis told us he then met Arthur Compeyson, who was good-looking and a smooth talker. Compeyson had gotten great wealth through some trick he'd played on a woman who loved him.

Compeyson was not a man to hold on to wealth long. He chose Provis as the man to help him gain more wealth. Together they swindled, forged, and took people's money in all ways short of bashing them on the head.

"Finally we both were caught and tried for one of our crimes," Provis said. "Compeyson's lawyer begged the jury to see it was all me and his client should not be punished."

They had both been sent to the prison ship, but with far different treatment. Provis plotted to get close to Compeyson. He attacked him for lying during the trial. Provis was thrown in the hold for it, but he managed to escape and swim for shore.

"I'd have made good my escape," the old man muttered. "But when you told me Compeyson was in the marshes, my freedom didn't matter to me. Only that he not be let free."

"Where is Compeyson now?" I asked.

"I don't know," Provis said. "Dead, I hope. If not, I'm sure he hopes me dead." And with that, the older man settled back, his eyes closed.

Herbert handed me a scrap of paper. I opened it and read: "Compeyson was the name of Miss Havisham's betrothed. He left her on her wedding day."

I became desperate to remove Provis from London. First, I was determined to see Estella and Miss Havisham. I learned Estella was visiting Miss Havisham and I left Provis in Herbert's charge to go see them both.

I arrived early in the morning and stopped at the inn for breakfast. I was annoyed to see Drummle there. I knew he must have come following Estella. Indeed he took great pains to mention to the staff at the inn that he would be dining at "the young lady's home."

Finally Drummle left. I saw him exchange words with a tattered man. The man looked a great deal like Orlick, but I assumed it was my imagination.

Finally, the morning grew late enough to call upon Miss Havisham's house. I was certain they knew about my mysterious benefactor, but I spoke of it anyway.

"Letting me believe you were my benefactor was unkind," I told Miss Havisham.

"When have you ever known me to be kind?" she answered.

I shrugged that off. "You have a chance to be kind," I said. "I will tell you now that your relatives, Herbert Pocket and his father, are not like the others. They do not scheme or covet. It would do you well to think of them differently."

She seemed to accept this, so I turned to Estella. "I love you," I said. "I am soon to be poor and have no claim to love you, yet I do. I need for you to know that."

Estella said she could not love me. She could not love anyone. Then she said the worst thing I could imagine. "I am going to be married to Bentley Drummle."

Nothing I said seemed to make a dent in her purpose. When I insisted he could not love her, she said that she could not love him either and that seemed fair.

I wept. I pleaded. But nothing would change her mind. As I lay my broken heart open before them, I saw deep pity in Miss Havisham's face. I believe she began to face what she had done with Estella's upbringing.

I left the house and set to walk the entire twenty-five miles to London. I could not bear the company of another person in my pain.

As I grew close to home, a watchman stopped me and pressed a note in my hand. I opened it and found Wemmick's writing plainly formed: "Don't go home."

CHAPTER
15

The Plan

I found a room for the night but slept little. My mind danced between the mystery of the note and the horror of Estella's marriage. When morning finally came, I headed straight out to see Wemmick and discover what his note was hiding.

I found Wemmick making breakfast for his aged parent. I helped with that as he talked in a low voice. He told me he heard that a certain person was missing in Australia. And being missing in Australia made certain people think that perhaps he was present in England. These very people now watched my rooms in hopes of finding this man.

"Who is looking for him?" I asked.

Wemmick would not say and I knew this must somehow conflict with his job. I could see that he had stepped out quite a ways to tell me as much as he did. I did not want to make things more difficult, but I had a question I needed answered.

"Have you heard of Compeyson?" I asked. "Is he alive?"

Wemmick nodded.

"Is he in London?" He gave me one more nod, then turned and I knew my questioning was over. Wemmick would say no more about who might be after Provis. But, he did tell me he and Herbert had discussed ways one might hide someone, should such a person ever need hiding.

They had decided that Provis should move into rooms in the house where Herbert's fiancée tended her elderly father. That way, Herbert could look after Provis's needs and carry messages without suspicion, since Herbert spent so much time there anyway.

The added benefit to the plan was that Clara's father lived right on the river, offering an easy escape. He looked at me directly then and said it might be best if we didn't try to escape immediately.

"There is no better place to hide than a great city once you are in it," he cautioned.

I agreed that this plan sounded best. Wemmick said he was glad I agreed, since the deed had already been done. I stayed at Wemmick's house until nightfall, then I left to check on Provis. I learned that everyone at the house thought Provis was named Campbell and that he was associated with Herbert and not with me.

This was my first meeting of Herbert's Clara. I knew she had thought me a poor companion for Herbert when he was in debt. Herbert assured me that her feelings had softened since he had found his calling at Clarriker's.

She was a charming girl, tiny with dark eyes. I thought she looked like a captive fairy, tending a grumpy ogre who roared frequently from upstairs. I found her a perfect match for Herbert, and their love for one another was clear.

After a pleasant visit with Clara, I climbed the stairs to see Provis. He seemed completely calm and content with the move.

"My coming here was an adventure, Pip," he said. "I'll enjoy it as such, whatever comes."

And so Provis was set in his new lodgings. Another plan was hatched where I would keep a boat on the river and be seen rowing for exercise. Then we might be unnoticed if we needed sudden escape in a boat.

When I left, I was surprised at how heavy my heart was to leave Provis behind. My feelings for him had softened. He had risked much in order to see me.

In the days ahead, I took up rowing as we'd planned. Soon no one took any notice of me as I rowed in good weather and bad. Sometimes

Herbert came with me. Still, I could not shake off a building anxiety.

Because I took no more money from Provis, my finances soon grew desperate. I sold jewelry to keep myself in food and lodging, but creditors pressed me for money. The sad turn in my finances could not compete with the constant worry that gnawed at me.

One evening after a long row on the river, I decided to find some light entertainment. I went to a shabby theater to watch a variety of short plays. Mr. Wopsle had become a London actor and he appeared in several of the plays. From his acting, I wondered if it might have been better if he had stayed a church clerk.

Still, it was pleasant to be reminded of the past. After the plays, I went backstage to visit. "Hello, Pip!" he cried and shook my hand. "I saw you in the audience. Who was that with you?"

"With me?" I felt a chill at the question.

"Ah, then you didn't know of the man," Wopsle said. "I wondered. He seemed so attached to you, almost like a ghost. Do you know whom he reminded me of?"

I could only shake my head, my throat thick with sudden fear.

"Do you remember the Christmas we dashed about the marshes looking for convicts?" Wopsle asked. "Remember when we found the men fighting?"

I nodded.

"This man reminded me of one of them," Wopsle said. "The one who was beaten. He looked so like him I would swear it was he."

The idea that Compeyson could be following me around made me still more afraid for Provis. Surely the time of greatest danger was near. From that moment, I made certain to row nowhere near the river house. I never turned so much as an eye in that direction.

Forgiveness

A few weeks after my ghostly encounter with Compeyson, I ran into Mr. Jaggers on the street. He invited me to dine with him. Since Mr. Wemmick would be there too, I agreed. Over dinner, Jaggers told me Miss Havisham had sent a note asking that I visit her.

I nodded. "I will go at once."

"So," said Mr. Jaggers, sitting back in his chair, "Drummle got his prize."

I nearly choked. My worst fear was realized. Estella had married him.

"It's hard to say who will be the stronger in that match," Jaggers said. "Drummle certainly cannot outthink her, but he is bigger."

I stared. "Surely he wouldn't hurt her?"

"He is the type," Jaggers said with a shrug. "Don't you think so, Wemmick?"

"The type," Wemmick agreed vaguely.

The subject was changed with the arrival of Jaggers's maid, Molly. He scolded her for slow service and she stood aside, watching us and twisting her hands nervously.

I stared at her face and recognition nudged at me. Suddenly I saw it. She looked very much like Estella. This was the orphan Estella's mother!

I fretted through the rest of dinner and was glad of my release at the end. I walked a bit with Wemmick and asked him to tell me Molly's story.

Wemmick told me that Molly was Mr. Jaggers's client many years ago in a murder trial. She'd married young to a man who was little more than a tramp. Somehow Molly had grown jealous of another woman and that woman had ended up dead.

"The murdered woman was ten years older than Molly and very much larger and stronger," Wemmick said. "Jaggers argued that Molly

couldn't possibly have killed such a woman. The murdered woman would have been a match for any man! He got her off the murder charge and she's worked for Mr. Jaggers ever since."

"Did she have a daughter?" I asked.

"Funny you should ask that," he said. "She did and some believed that she killed her own child as well. There was no evidence of it. The child was gone sure enough, disappeared, and her just three years old."

I departed the next morning to see Miss Havisham. She was not in her dressing room, but sat in the larger room across the hall staring into an ashy fire. I greeted her gently, for she looked profoundly lonely.

"Are you real?" she whispered.

"I am," I said. "I got your letter yesterday and here I am."

"Thank you." Her eyes wandered back to the fire. I pulled a chair over to the fire and waited. Finally she looked at me and said, "My heart is not completely stone. I would like to help Herbert. How much more needs to be paid to make him a partner?"

I hesitated. "Nine hundred pounds."

"I will give it, but in secret," she said. "Will you forgive me, Pip? Someday when I am decayed bones, do you think you will forgive me?"

"I forgive you now," I said, taking her cold hands in mine. "You have made mistakes, but so have we all."

"At first, I meant only to save an orphan child from my own misery," Miss Havisham said. "But I could not keep that motive." She sobbed.

"Miss Havisham," I said softly, "how old was Estella when she came to you?"

"She was two or three," she said. "Mr. Jaggers found her for me."

Soon after that, I left Miss Havisham to her lonely room. I wandered the grounds before deciding it was time for me to seek out a place for the night.

I looked back toward the house and was struck with an uneasy feeling that I should check on Miss Havisham. So I did. She was still seated in the chair, facing the fire and seemed well.

Just then, a log shifted and the fire roared up. Miss Havisham was too close and the fire caught at her. She ran toward me, shrieking. I threw my heavy cloak over her and dragged the tablecloth off the rotting table to add to the fabric smothering the flames.

Servants ran in then. Miss Havisham was badly burned, her clothes in black cinders. A doctor came. He said the burns should heal, if she survived the shock.

As the doctor spoke, I saw my own hands were burned. I had been so caught up in worry, I had not noticed. I knew I could do nothing else there. So I left to return to the city.

Looping Back

My bandaged hands ached badly, though I still had some use of my right hand. Herbert cared for me kindly, changing bandages and soaking them in a cooling liquid.

"I've talked much with Provis," Herbert said. "He told me the most astounding story about a woman from his past. Shall I tell you?"

"Please do," I said, eager for anything to take my mind off my pain.

Herbert launched into the tale as he changed my bandages yet again, "The young woman had been outrageously jealous of anyone Provis turned an eye toward—jealous enough to murder. She killed a woman, though Jaggers got her off on the charge."

I jumped, amazed that again things in my life had looped back upon themselves. "Tell me more," I said.

"The murder wasn't the worst of it," Herbert said. "There was a child, a daughter, that Provis was deeply fond of. The woman declared she would destroy it in revenge. Neither woman nor child was seen again by Provis."

It seemed impossible but I was certain. "Herbert," I said, "the man we have in hiding down the river is Estella's father."

As soon as I was able, I went to Mr. Jaggers to have my suspicions confirmed. Though he talked in circles, I followed well enough to see that Estella was the child of Provis and Molly.

"Now, if such a secret did exist," Jaggers said, "who would benefit from making it known? Would the father feel better? Some secrets ought to be kept for the good of all."

I did not know if I agreed with that, but I could think of no argument. After seeing Mr. Jaggers, I paid for Herbert's partnership with

Miss Havisham's money. I felt much improved for having helped my dear friend.

Over the next month, my arms healed until I could use them slightly. Then we received the note from Wemmick. The time had come to sneak Provis out of England.

Herbert and I studied foreign steamers, certain that one of them would be the best way to get Provis out of the country. All we needed to do was get him aboard.

We decided to call in the aid of our old friend Startop. He could take my half of the rowing while Herbert took the other half. I would steer. We would row up to the house where Provis stayed and load him into the boat on the back stairs.

After settling the plan, I went home to discover a note waiting for me. It bade me come to the marshes that night. The writer had information about my uncle Provis. I left a note for Herbert and rushed to catch a coach once again for my old home.

It was dark when I arrived. A full moon offered some light. I wandered for a bit, meeting no one. Finally I came to a small shack.

I knocked and no one answered. I tried the latch and slipped inside. "Is there anyone here?" I called. Suddenly I was caught from behind.

"Now I've got you," a voice cried.

I fought, but with my arms still weak there was little I could do. The man soon tied me up. It was then that I knew him, Orlick.

"You ruined my life," he called. "Joe was all for you. You stood between me and Biddy, too." He slammed a hand on the table. "And I know you ended my job at the mansion."

"What will you do to me?" I asked.

"The same I did for your shrew sister," he replied.

I yelled then, yelled with all my might. To my amazement, my cries were answered. A small group of men burst through the door and jumped on Orlick. They wrestled him to the ground. One of the men broke from the group to rush to my side. It was Herbert!

At seeing my scrawled note, he had come following me. Startop too. They had pulled in men from town, including the tailor's boy. I was glad to see him now.

Together we returned to London to complete our plan for saving Provis. I rested all the day to regain my strength for the night ahead.

CHAPTER 18

The Trial

The plan was simple. We would row a bit to be certain no one had an unhealthy interest in us. Then we would pick up Provis and find a spot to wait out the night. In the morning, we would flag down the steamer headed to Hamburg. If they refused to pick us up, there was another headed for Rotterdam that should work as well. Once aboard, we should be safe.

I felt some relief at the plan finally being under way. I was of little use, but I found the fresh morning air brought a sense of hope.

The river was busy with small boats. Time passed quickly and soon I spotted the Mill Pond stairs. We touched the stairs lightly for a moment and Provis was aboard.

I scanned the water for any sign of being suspected. Provis was the least anxious of any of us.

"If all goes well, you will be free and safe in a few hours," I said.

He drew a long breath. "I hope so."

We rowed throughout the day. When dark settled on us, we looked for a lonely tavern to tie up. In the darkness, we jumped at every noise, certain we were finally being followed.

We found a very dirty public house that would rent us two rooms. We pulled the boat ashore for the night and went in.

We ate and slept and planned what time to put the boat back in the water. We decided to wait until within an hour of the time the steamer should pass. We put in the water then, to limit our time out in the open.

When we set out the next day, our only concern was a galley rowing along the river. We drew up alongside it, as it seemed unwise to be seen avoiding it. The men in the boat stared at us. In the middle of the boat, a man sat bundled up much as Provis was.

We rowed alongside one another until we spotted the steamer. It grew very near us. Suddenly someone from the galley cried out, "That man in the cloak is Abel Magwitch. I call upon him to surrender and all of you in the boat to assist."

They ran the galley against us and grabbed hold of our small boat. I saw Provis stand up and grab the cloak from the bundled man in the galley. It was Compeyson.

The men wrestled, bridging out the two boats until our small boat was overturned. Startop, Herbert, and I splashed in the water. Eventually I spotted Provis as he was hauled into the galley and shackled. There was nothing we could do, so we swam to shore and made our way back to the public house.

Soon the galley tied up at the public house, too. Magwitch was injured and needed care. Apparently he attacked Compeyson again and had driven them both overboard. They fought more under the water. Magwitch said he was then struck by the passing steamer. He remembered nothing else, though obviously his captor had retrieved him.

As I held his hand, he smiled at me. "My boy will have to go on and be a gentleman without me," he said. "You should go now and not be seen with me."

"I'll not leave your side unless forced," I said.

And so I stayed. There was little doubt as to Magwitch's fate, only whether he would live long enough to be executed. Compeyson was eventually found. He had drowned.

During the horrible weeks of waiting for Magwitch's fate, Herbert told me he had to leave London. He was to open a new branch of the business in Cairo. He offered me a position there as a clerk.

I told him I could not leave Magwitch and asked if the offer would remain open for a while. Herbert agreed.

Magwitch grew weaker as his trial approached. He had broken ribs and injured his lungs. His breathing grew worse and worse. He lay in the prison infirmary and I was allowed to visit for a few hours each day.

The day for the trial came. Magwitch was hauled into court and propped up in a chair. There was no doubt that he had returned to England and that returning meant death. His trial was brief.

He returned to the infirmary to await the carrying out of the sentence. I continued to visit every day. Then one day, he gripped my hand with some of his old enthusiasm. "Thankee, dear boy. You've never deserted me."

Then he seemed to lose his strength at once and I knew the time had come. I leaned close to him.

"You had a child once, whom you loved and lost," I said softly. He squeezed my hand to show he had heard. "She lived and grew to be a lady and very beautiful. I love her."

With that, he raised my hand to his lips and kissed it. Then his hand went slack and he was gone.

Friends

After that, an illness struck me down. I fell upon my sofa and slipped in and out of feverish dreams. Dear Joe entered my dreams more and more. Then one day, I awoke to a strong arm around me, holding a cup of water to my lips. I sank back after a few sips and stared.

"Is it Joe?" I asked.

"It is," he said, smiling kindly.

"Don't smile," I gasped. "Strike me. Yell at me. Curse me for the knave I am."

"You and me are ever friends, dear old Pip," he said.

As he took care of me, he told me how he had come as soon as he heard I was sick. He told me Biddy had insisted that he must.

He had other news as well. Miss Havisham had finally passed away from her burns. She left a sum of money to Herbert's father.

"She said in the will that she left the money because you spoke so well of him," Joe said.

With the days and weeks of my illness, the years fell away between Joe and I. But as I grew stronger, it seemed Joe backed away.

Then one morning, I woke to find a note lying on the table in Joe's careful scrawl: "I have departed, for you are well again and will do better without."

I decided that I must follow Joe and show him I was well and truly still his Pip. I would propose to Biddy, for she was a far worthier woman than I deserved. I would spend no more time thinking myself a gentleman.

I rested three more days to be sure I had the strength, then I headed to my old home. I found Joe and Biddy in the parlor, each dressed in their very best. They were delighted at the sight of me.

"You've come for our wedding day," Biddy said in a burst of joy. "I am married to Joe."

And at that, I fainted. They carried me in to the kitchen and fussed over me. Finally I was recovered enough to speak. "Dear Biddy, you have the best husband in the world," I said.

"I do," Biddy agreed.

"And, dear Joe, you have the best wife in the whole world. I hope that you will have children to love," I said. "I am sure any son of the two of you would grow up a better man than I."

Joe insisted that could not be so. I told them then I was going abroad to join Herbert's company as a clerk. I promised to repay the money that Joe had spent to pay my debts. I begged their forgiveness for my actions over the years to both of them.

They forgave me, and I found myself more content than I had been at any point in my riches.

I sold everything I had and paid what I could to my remaining creditors with plans to pay the rest from my new position. Herbert married Clara and I lived with them so that I could pay my debts.

Eventually I became a partner in the firm. Clarriker said he could keep the secret no longer. He told my part in Herbert's fortunes. Herbert received it as proof of friendship and we continued the better for it.

For eleven years I lived away. Finally I could take a moment for myself, and I returned to visit Joe and Biddy. I found a small son with them.

"We gave him the name of Pip for your sake, old chap," Joe said.

During my visit, Biddy asked if I thought much of Estella. "I am no longer sick for wanting her," I said. I knew Estella's life had been hard with Drummle. I'd heard of his death two years before in a riding accident after beating his horse. Beyond that, I knew nothing. I assumed Estella had married again.

Talk of Estella made me long to see the mansion again. I took a walk to see what had become of it and found it gone. No house. No building whatsoever. Just a cleared space.

It was a misty evening as I walked around the rocks and weeds. I spotted a figure in the mists. As I approached it, I heard my name.

"Estella," I called out.

"I am greatly changed," she said. "It's a wonder you know me."

The freshness of her beauty was gone but so was the cold pride. We sat together and talked about the house and about my work.

"I have often thought of you," she said.

"And you have always held a place in my heart," I answered.

"I wish you could forgive me," she said. "Before we part again, I wish we could be friends."

"We are friends," I said and I stood, pulling her from the bench and walking in the mist with her. And though I looked about, I saw no shadow of another parting from her.